Nightgown Countdown

Written by Frank B. Edwards
Illustrated by John Bianchi

. . . NINE.

Nine farm animals prancing past the gate.
Pig felt tired, then there were . . .

. . . EIGHT.
Eight farm animals clattering close to heaven.
Sheep slipped and fell, then there were . . .

. . . SEVEN.
Seven farm animals getting lots of kicks.
Dog lay down, then there were . . .

. . . SIX.

Six farm animals hopping around the hive.

Goat bumped a bee, then there were . . .

. . . FIVE.

Five farm animals bouncing on the floor.

Cow made a hole, then there were . . .

. . .FOUR.
Four farm animals climbing up a tree.
Cat went too high, then there were . . .

. . . THREE.
Three farm animals stepping around some poo.
Rat slipped and fell, then there were . . .

. . . TWO.
Two farm animals waiting for the sun.
Hen fell asleep, then there was . . .

. . . ONE.

One farm animal looking for his friends . . .

...the end.